Dear Parents,

Welcome to the Scholastic Reader series. We have taken over 80 years of experience with teachers, parents, and children and put it into a program that is designed to match your child's interests and skills.

Level 1—Short sentences and stories made up of words kids can sound out using their phonics skills and words that are important to remember.

Level 2—Longer sentences and stories with words kids need to know and new "big" words that they will want to know.

Level 3—From sentences to paragraphs to longer stories, these books have large "chunks" of texts and are made up of a rich vocabulary.

Level 4—First chapter books with more words and fewer pictures.

It is important that children learn to read well enough to succeed in school and beyond. Here are ideas for reading this book with your child:

- Look at the book together. Encourage your child to read the title and make a prediction about the story.
- Read the book together. Encourage your child to sound out words when appropriate. When your child struggles, you can help by providing the word.
- Encourage your child to retell the story. This is a great way to check for comprehension.
- Have your child take the fluency test on the last page to check progress.

Scholastic Readers are designed to support your child's efforts to learn how to read at every age and every stage. Enjoy helping your child learn to read and love to read.

—**Francie Alexander**
Chief Education Officer
Scholastic Education

ISBN 0-439-47099-4

Copyright © 2004 by DC Comics.
Batman and all related characters and elements
are trademarks of and © DC Comics.
All rights reserved. Published by Scholastic Inc.
SCHOLASTIC, CARTWHEEL BOOKS, and associated logos are
trademarks and/or registered trademarks of Scholastic Inc.

Library of Congress Cataloging-in-Publication data is available.

10 9 8 7 6 5 4 3 2 1   04 05 06 07 08

Printed in the U.S.A. 23 • First printing, November 2004

THE BIRTHDAY BASH

Written by **Percival Muntz**

Illustrated by **Rick Burchett**

Batman created by Bob Kane

Scholastic Reader — Level 3

Cartwheel
·B·O·O·K·S· ®

SCHOLASTIC INC.

New York Toronto London Auckland Sydney
Mexico City New Delhi Hong Kong Buenos Aires

CHAPTER ONE

MISSING: ONE CLOWN

Bruce Wayne was one of the richest men in Gotham City. He lived in Wayne Manor, above a secret cave — the Batcave!

That's because Bruce was also Batman!

Every evening, Batman carefully checked his crime-fighting tools and equipment. Then he would go out on patrol.

It was late afternoon in Gotham City. The Batmobile came to a stop in front of Arkham Asylum. Commissioner Gordon stood waiting as Batman climbed out of the car.

"Bad news, Batman," said Gordon.

"Has there been a breakout?" asked Batman.

"Follow me," Gordon said.

Loud laughs and angry shouts filled the dark hallways inside Arkham. Behind closed doors were the mean villains Batman had caught during his many adventures.

THE JOKER HAS **ESCAPED!**

The commissioner and the Dark Knight walked to an open door at the end of the hall.

"It's worse than I thought," said Batman. "This was the Joker's cell!"

Gordon pointed to a big hole in the wall. Smoke rose from the hole.

"How did this happen?" asked Batman.

"The Joker had been very good lately," Gordon said. "So we let him bake a cake in the kitchen."

"He must have mixed something with the flour and sugar to make a bomb," said Batman.

"Right," agreed Gordon. "When he went back to his cell, he put a candle in the cake, lit it, and *BOOM*!"

"A candle?" asked Batman. "That's right! It's the Joker's birthday. I bet I know where he's gone, too!"

CHAPTER TWO

FUN-HOUSE FIGHT

On Gotham Pier, an amusement park
stood empty. The rides had been closed long
ago. Now they were falling apart.

At the entrance to the park, an old sign
read DANGER—KEEP OUT! But in the back

room of the Fun House, two men played a game of checkers. One man was named Sweeny. The other was named McGurk.

Sweeny looked up from the game. "Do you think our boss really broke out of Arkham Asylum?" he asked.

McGurk shook his head. "He said to meet him here tonight. But no one breaks out of that place."

A laugh came from the shadows. Sweeny and McGurk jumped up, knocking over the checkerboard. "I'm glad you boys really believed in me!" said a familiar voice.

SWEENY AND MCGURK HEARD THE JOKER!

The Joker walked into the room in his
Arkham Asylum uniform.

"I'm back, boys! And it's my birthday!
Breaking out of Arkham was a treat, but I
want a real party and presents!"

The Joker opened a closet. Inside was a

row of purple suits. He put one on. Then he pressed a flower on his lapel. The flower squirted water right into McGurk's face!

Then the Joker threw a newspaper to Sweeny. On the front page was an article about an emerald.

"The Emerald of Ghulpar is owned by the rich Van Guilders," the Joker said. "They are throwing a birthday party for their son tonight. We're going to crash the party and get that emerald!"

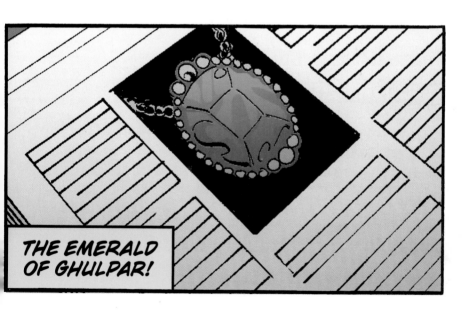

THE EMERALD OF GHULPAR!

"That's all I needed to hear!" boomed another voice.

"No!" shouted the Joker. "How did you find me so quickly?"

"You shouldn't have returned to your old hideout!" said Batman.

"Get him!" screamed the Joker.

Sweeny and McGurk lunged for Batman. But two Batarangs spun out of the darkness and knocked the goons to the ground. Then the Joker ran through a door. Batman was close behind.

CHAPTER THREE

HERE'S LOOKING AT YOU

"Where is the Joker?" Batman wondered. Everywhere he looked, he only saw his own reflection. Batman had walked into the Hall of Mirrors.

"Yoo-hoo, Bats!" A shrill voice echoed in the room. "I bet you can't find me!"

Suddenly, Batman saw the Joker. Batman reached out to grab him. But instead his fist broke a mirror. He looked around. Images of the Joker were all around him. But which one was real?

Batman grabbed for another image. But a second mirror broke into a hundred pieces. Batman could hear the Joker laughing.

"How are you going to catch me if you don't know which me is the real me?" asked the Joker.

Then the real Joker crept up behind Batman. He hit Batman hard with his fist. Batman fell to the floor in a heap.

CHAPTER FOUR

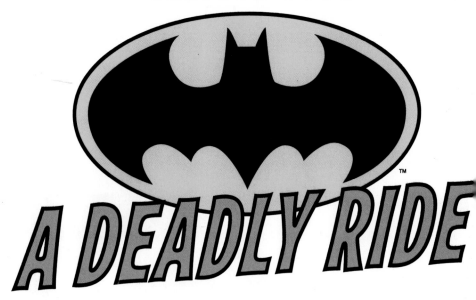

A DEADLY RIDE

When Batman woke up, he found he was chained to a seat on the old Ferris wheel.

"Enjoy the ride!" said the Joker.

He pushed a lever. Slowly, the Ferris wheel began to shake and creak.

"I've set this rusty ride to go as fast as it can!" said the Joker. "So long, Batman! I have a birthday bash to crash!" And the Joker and his men ran off into the night.

BATMAN WAS CHAINED TO THE RUSTY FERRIS WHEEL.

As the Ferris wheel turned, Batman was lifted up into the sky. He could see Gotham City's lights in the distance.

Then the city turned upside down and back upright again as the Ferris wheel began to spin faster and faster. The view of Gotham City became a blur. Suddenly, the ride shook and swayed.

"This ride is going to fall off its base," said Batman. "And then it will roll right into the sea, taking me with it!"

GOTHAM CITY WAS A BLUR...

BATMAN TRIED TO **ESCAPE THE CHAINS.**

CHAPTER FIVE

HAPPY BIRTHDAY, JOKER!

The Van Guilder estate was huge. Long green lawns were covered with streamers and balloons. Colored lights shone in every tree. And there was a banner that read: HAPPY BIRTHDAY, GASPAR.

Gaspar and his friends were on the patio. They wore party hats and tooted on noisemakers. Next to Gaspar was a huge stack of presents.

EDITH VAN GUILDER WORE THE EMERALD NECKLACE.

Vincent Van Guilder stood with Edith Van Guilder and watched the children.

"You look lovely, dear," said Vincent.

Edith wore a nice gown and a necklace with a beautiful emerald set in the center. Edith touched her hand to the emerald and smiled.

At that very moment, the gate swung open. A tall, thin man in a purple suit walked into the yard. There were two large men behind him. With a crazy smile on his face, the tall man walked up to the Van Guilders.

"Are you the birthday clown?" asked Gaspar.

The Joker turned to the boy. "Some know me as the Clown Prince of Crime. But I prefer to be called…the Joker!"

THE CLOWN PRINCE OF CRIME…THE JOKER!

VINCENT TRIED TO LUNGE FOR THE JOKER.

I'LL TAKE THAT EMERALD!

Everyone gasped. The Joker pointed to Edith. "I'll take that emerald!"

Vincent tried to lunge for the Joker. But he was no match for Sweeny and McGurk, who had their arms around him.

Edith clutched the emerald. "Please don't take this—it was a present from my husband."

"Well, now it's *my* birthday present!" said the Joker with an evil laugh. He snatched the emerald from her throat. "Sweeny, McGurk. It's time to have some fun!"

"But, boss," said Sweeny, "you got your emerald. Shouldn't we get out of here?"

"No!" shouted the Joker. "Batman won't ever bother us again. And my birthday party is just about to start!"

CHAPTER SIX

SINK OR SWIM?

Back at Gotham Pier, the Ferris wheel spun faster and faster. Batman heard bolts and screws popping loose below him. He had to think fast! Suddenly, the Ferris wheel broke off its base and began rolling down the pier.

As Batman went head over heels, he slipped his fingers into his Utility Belt. He grabbed his cutting torch and lit it. Then he burned

BATMAN WAS IN TROUBLE...

through the chains that held him.

When the Ferris wheel reached the end of the pier, the wheel and Batman plunged into

THE WHEEL SANK
INTO THE OCEAN!

SPLASH

BUT BATMAN
ESCAPED!

the dark, icy waters of the ocean!

A second later, Batman pulled himself back onto the pier, dripping wet. He had broken free!

As Batman sped away in his Batmobile, he called Commissioner Gordon.

"I know where the Joker is, Commissioner," said Batman. "But he'll be with lots of children. I have to get him without putting the kids in danger."

"How will you do that?" asked Gordon.

"I'm going to stop at a bakery on the way," said Batman, and he smiled.

"Batman!" exclaimed Gordon. "This is no time for dessert!"

CHAPTER SEVEN

SWEET SURPRISE!

THE JOKER STOLE GASPAR'S NEW BIKE!

At the Van Guilder home, the Joker was ruining the party. Gaspar watched as the Joker rode around and around the yard on Gaspar's new bicycle, singing, "Happy birthday to me!"

"That bike is mine!" said Gaspar.

"Not anymore, Gas-boy!" said the Joker.

"I don't like you at all," said Gaspar. "You're an awful birthday clown!" He and his friends stuck out their tongues at the Joker.

Just then, a deliveryman put a very large birthday cake on the front yard and then drove away.

The Joker grinned at Vincent and Edith. "You ordered a surprise birthday cake all for me? Bring it here, boys!"

Mr. and Mrs. Van Guilder looked at each other. Neither of them had ordered a cake this big.

Sweeny and McGurk pushed the cake right up to the Joker. "Light the candles!" cried the Clown Prince of Crime. "I want to make a birthday wish!"

Suddenly, the top of the cake flew off! Out popped Batman from inside!

"It'll be your last wish, Joker!" said Batman. As fast as lightning, he threw two Batarangs.

"Not again!" said Sweeny.

"I hate those things!" said McGurk.

The Batarangs wrapped around the goons, and they fell with a *THUD*!

"I'm not going to let you ruin my birthday party!" the Joker shouted. And he ran toward Batman.

Batman swung his leg in a flying kick. The Joker stumbled. Then Gaspar put out his leg, tripping the villain. The Joker fell hard into his own birthday cake! *SPLAT*!

CHAPTER EIGHT

THE LAST LAUGH?

Outside the mansion, Batman gave the emerald back to Mrs. Van Guilder.

Then he walked over to the patrol car. "Looks like you'll be celebrating many birthdays at Arkham Asylum, Joker," said Batman.

"Wrong, Bats!" said the Joker. "I'll be out again soon. You know why? Because I've decided my birthday's really next week! Ha! Ha! Ha! Ha!"

The Joker's crazy laugh echoed into the night as the patrol car drove away.

Fluency Fun

The words in each list below end in the same sounds.
Read the words in a list.
Read them again.
Read them faster.
Try to read all 15 words in one minute.

amazement	**awfully**	**commission**
amusement	**carefully**	**joker**
development	**lately**	**newspaper**
equipment	**quickly**	**noisemaker**
moment	**suddenly**	**streamer**

Look for these words in the story.

adventure	**villain**	**familiar**
beautiful	**laugh**	

Note to Parents:

According to *A Dictionary of Reading and Related Terms*, fluency is "the ability to read smoothly, easily, and readily with freedom from word-recognition problems." Fluency is necessary for good comprehension and enjoyable reading. The activities on this page include a speed drill and a sight-recognition drill. Speed drills build fluency because they help students rapidly recognize common syllables and spelling patterns in words, and they're fun! Sight-recognition drills help students smoothly and accurately recognize words. Practice these activities with your child to help him or her become a fluent reader.

—Wiley Blevins,
Reading Specialist